Robin Hill School

Secret Santa

written by Margaret McNamara
illustrated by Mike Gordon

Ready-to-Read

Simon Spotlight

New York   London   Toronto   Sydney   New Delhi

For Becky, because she loves Christmas —M. M.

Simon Spotlight
An imprint of Simon & Schuster Children's Publishing Division
1230 Avenue of the Americas, New York, NY 10020
Text copyright © 2012 by Margaret McNamara
Illustrations copyright © 2012 by Mike Gordon
For information about special discounts for bulk purchases, please contact Simon & Schuster Special Sales at 1-866-506-1949 or business@simonandschuster.com.
0812 LAK
2 4 6 8 10 9 7 5 3 1
Library of Congress Cataloging-in-Publication Data
McNamara, Margaret.
Secret Santa / by Margaret McNamara ; illustrated by Mike Gordon. – 1st ed.
p. cm. – (Robin Hill School) (Ready-to-read)
Summary: When Katie draws Andrew's name in the first-grade Christmas gift exchange, she decides not to give him a present because he has said mean things about her reindeer sweater.
ISBN 978-1-4424-3648-0 (pbk. : alk. paper)
ISBN 978-1-4424-3649-7 (hardcover : alk. paper)
ISBN 978-1-4424-3650-3 (eBook)
[1. Gifts—Fiction. 2. Behavior--Fiction. 3. Schools—Fiction. 4. Christmas—Fiction.] I. Gordon, Mike, 1948 Mar. 16- ill. II. Title.
PZ7.M47879343Sec 2012   [E] —dc23   2011027463

Today was Secret Santa Day at Robin Hill School.

Katie wore
her Christmas sweater.
She skipped into class.

"That reindeer
looks like a raccoon,"
said Andrew.
Katie stopped skipping.

"Secret Santa time," said Mrs. Connor. She gave each student a piece of paper.

"We write our names," said James.

"We fold the paper,"
said Eigen.

"We put them in
the Santa hat," said Ayanna.

"Rudolph Raccoon,"
Andrew whispered to Katie.

"You are mean,"
Katie whispered back.

"Close your eyes
and pick a name,"
said Mrs. Connor.

When it was Katie's turn,
she made a wish.
"I hope I do not
get Andrew," she thought.
She got Andrew.

At home that night
Katie told her mom
what Andrew had said.

"I will not
get Andrew a present,"
said Katie.
"Hmm," said her mom.

The next day,
everyone talked
about their presents.

"I will give Hannah a mug!"
said Jamie.

"I know what I will give Becky!" said Eigen.

"I will give Nick a car!"
said Nia.
Katie did not
say anything.

On Monday, Katie's mom
gave her a present
for Andrew.
But Katie did not
take it to school.

When it was almost time
to give out presents,
Katie started to cry.

"What is wrong?"
asked Mrs. Connor.
"I do not have
a present for Andrew,"
said Katie.

"He was mean

so I wanted to be mean too.

But now I want to be nice."

"We have time
to make a present together,"
said Mrs. Connor.

They went to the craft corner
and began to
make something.

At last it was time
for presents.
Jamie got a pencil case.

Reza got a pen
with four colors.

Katie opened her present.

It was a reindeer.

"Sorry," said Andrew.

"And merry Christmas!"

Katie gave Andrew his
present.

It was a raccoon.

"Sorry," said Katie.

"And merry Christmas!"

Hannah loved her mug.

Becky loved her book.

Nick loved his car.

But Andrew and Katie
loved their presents
best of all.